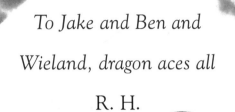

To Jake and Ben and

Wieland, dragon aces all

R. H.

Text copyright © 1980 by the Estate of Russell Hoban
Illustrations copyright © 1980, 2015 by Quentin Blake

First U.S. edition 2015

Library of Congress Catalog Card Number 2013957524
ISBN 978-0-7636-7482-3

15 16 17 18 19 20 CCP 10 9 8 7 6 5 4 3 2 1

Printed in Shenzhen, Guangdong, China

This book was typeset in Goudy Old Style.
The illustrations were done in watercolor and ink.

Candlewick Press
99 Dover Street
Somerville, Massachusetts 02144

visit us at www.candlewick.com

ACE DRAGON LTD.

Russell Hoban
& Quentin Blake

CANDLEWICK PRESS

John was walking down the street when he heard something go *KLONK*.

John looked down and saw a round iron plate in the pavement. It was like a manhole cover. On it he read: ACE DRAGON LTD. John stamped three times on the iron cover.

A voice said, "Who is it?"

John said, "John."

The voice said, "What do you want?"

John said, "I want to know what LTD. means."

The voice said, "It means limited."

John said, "What does *limited* mean?"

The voice said, "It means I can't do everything. I can only do some things."

John said, "What can you do?"

The voice said, "I can make fire come out of my nose and mouth. I can fly. I can spin gold into straw if you have any gold."

John said, "I don't have any gold."

The voice said, "Do you need any straw?"

John said, "No."

The voice said, "Then it doesn't matter. Do you want to go flying with me?"

John said, "Yes, I do."

The voice said, "Then you have to come down and fight me. If you win, I'll take you flying."

John said, "I can't lift this iron cover.
It's too heavy. Can you lift it?"

The voice said, "No, I can't."

John said, "How can we meet, then?"

The voice said, "Take the Underground to
Dragonham East. I'll meet you there."

John said, "How shall I know you?"

The voice said, "I'll be wearing two pairs
of Wellingtons. How shall I know you?"

John said, "I'll have a sword."

The voice said, "See you then."

John said, "See you."

John took the Underground to Dragonham East. There he saw a dragon in Wellingtons.

The ace dragon said, "How do you do?
I'm Ace Dragon Ltd."
John said, "How do you do? I'm John."

Ace and John found an abandoned lot, and got ready to fight.

Ace said, "Best out of three?"
John said, "Right."

Ace and John had their first fight.

John won.

Ace and John had their second fight.

John won.

John said, "That's two in a row.

That's best out of three. Now you have to take
me flying."

John got on Ace's back, and off they flew.

Ace and John flew very high and very far.
John said to Ace, "Can you do stunts? Can
you do sky-writing with fire?"

Ace did stunts and sky-writing with fire.

They were very high up and it was getting dark when Ace said, "I'm running out of petrol."

John said, "I didn't know you ran on petrol."

Ace said, "That's how I make my fire, and that's what makes me go. I've used up so much petrol with the sky-writing that we don't have enough to get us back."

John said, "Can't we glide back down to earth?"

Ace said, "No, we can't. If I stop flapping my wings, we'll crash, and it's a very long way down."

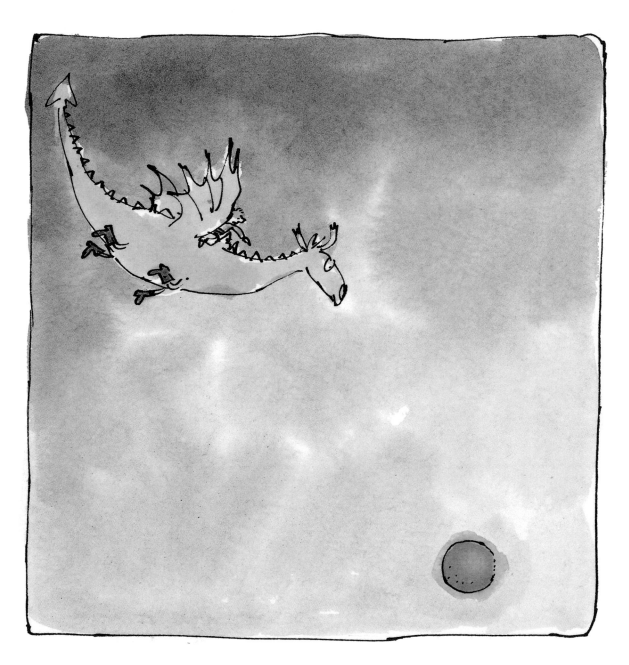

John said, "Look! There's a little golden moon below us. Can you get that far?"

Ace said, "I'll try."

They landed on the moon just as Ace ran
out of petrol.

John said, "We could jump back down to
earth if we had something soft to land on."

Ace said, "Yes, but we don't have
something soft to land on."

John said, "This is a golden moon."
He sliced off some gold with his sword.
John said to Ace, "If you can spin gold
into straw, you can make something soft
for us to land on."

Ace spun the gold into straw. Then John sliced
off more gold, and Ace spun more into straw.

Ace and John made a
great big bundle of straw.

Then they held on to the bundle as they jumped.

THUMP! They landed safely in the middle of the abandoned lot.

Ace said, "I have to go home for supper now."
John said, "So do I. You know what, Ace?"
Ace said, "What?"
John said, "You're not so limited."

Ace said, "Thanks. I'll see you."
John said, "See you."

Then they both
went home for
supper.

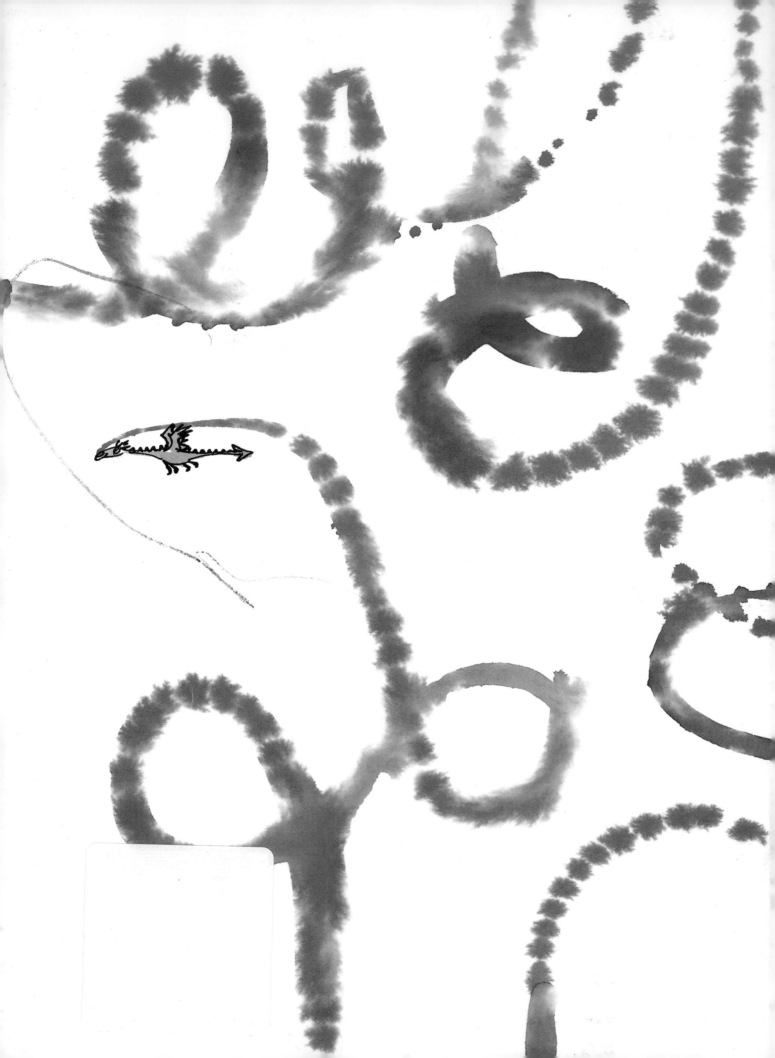